Foreword

I first met Maynard Moose one foggy morning years ago in downeast Maine. He was sitting on a mossy log, telling stories to a chipmunk and a crow. Pure chance had led me down that path—chance and great good fortune. For I had stumbled upon the last living teller of Mother Moose Tales—those strange and magical stories sent down by Mother Moose herself so long ago.

I visited Maynard many times over the following months, and finally gathered the courage to ask him if I might record his tales for posterity. He readily agreed, and I began to make a series of field recordings, hoping to one day make the stories into books.

When the time came to translate Maynard's tales into print, however, I faced unexpected difficulties. Moose language (even Modern Moose) has its own laws and rhythms, quite different in many ways from human speech. And as you will hear on the enclosed CD, moose do not pronounce words quite the way that we do. The moose substitution of the *th* sound for *s*, for example, made translating Maynard's voice to the page especially challenging. In the end, we decided to humanize Maynard's pronunciation, but to keep the original Moose vocabulary intact. We hope that the addition of hoofnotes (❜) will help make Maynard's meanings clear. And those unfamiliar with the cadences of moose speech will find the enclosed field recording a useful guide when reading aloud.

May all humans discover, and discover once more, the joys of gathering together to hear the old tales told again.

—Willy Claflin

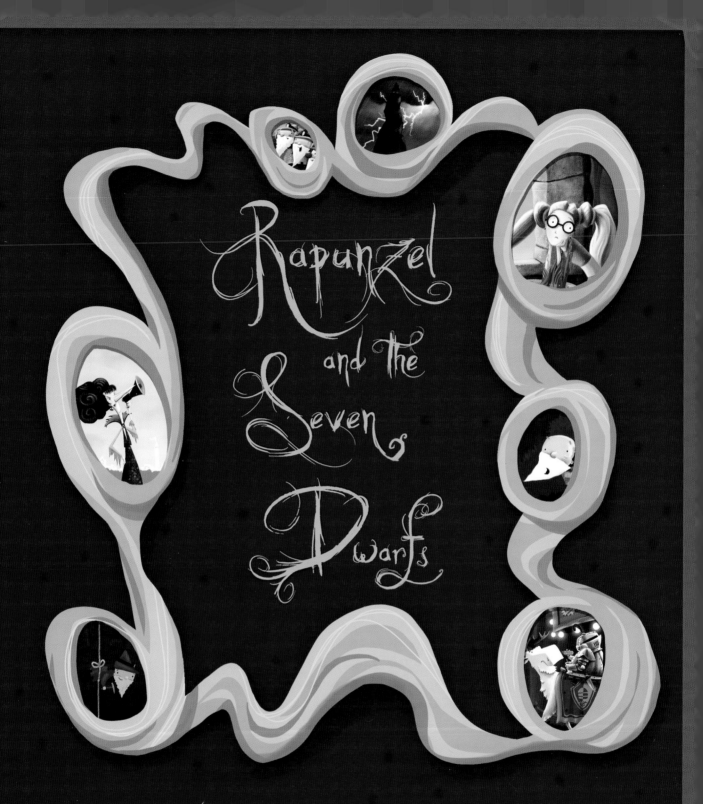

Rapunzel and the Seven Dwarfs

A Maynard Moose Tale
As told to Willy Claflin

Illustrated by James Stimson

AUGUST HOUSE
Little folk

For Jacqueline Darrigrand, Moose Muse.
—W.C.

For the wind in the wood, and the stars
in the night.
—M.M.

For Ingrid, your inspiration and your
understanding.

- J.S.

Text copyright © 2011 by Willy Claflin
Illustrations copyright © 2011 by James Stimson

Book design by Graham Anthony
Audio CD recording, music, and voice-over introduction by Brian Claflin

Printed by Pacom Korea
Seoul, South Korea
December 2010

10 9 8 7 6 5 4 3 2 1

Published 2011 by August House LittleFolk
3500 Piedmont Road NE, Suite 310, Atlanta, Georgia 30305
404-442-4420
www.augusthouse.com

LIBRARY OF CONGRESS CATALOGING-IN-PUBLICATION DATA

Claflin, Willy, 1944-
 Rapunzel and the seven dwarfs : a Maynard Moose tale / Willy Claflin ; illustrated by James Stimson.
  p. cm.
 Summary: Combines and resets the classic tales of Rapunzel and Snow White in the Northern Piney Woods of Maine, where a prince riding a white moose tries to rescue a long-haired beauty who has been poisoned by a witch.
 ISBN 978-0-87483-914-2 (hardcover : alk. paper)
 [1. Fairy tales.] I. Stimson, James, ill. II. Rapunzel. English. III. Snow White and the seven dwarfs. English. IV. Title.
 PZ8.C498Rap 2011
 [E]--dc22
                              2009052941

AUGUST HOUSE, INC.
ATLANTA

Glossary and Hoofnotes
Moose Words and Their English Equivalents

Parental Warning! This book contains moose grammar, spelling, and usage, all of which have been known to scrumble up the human brain!

Although this text has been painstakingly translated from the original Moose, it contains many traces of Piney Woods English, a dialect generally used by Aroostic County Mooses in northern Maine. Piney Woods words have been designated by hoofnotes (❛❜) in the text, and are defined below.

Amunals: animals, especially furry animals of the Northern Piney Woods

Angrified: angry

Branglebush: A bush that grows in the Northern Piney Woods. Its stickers are so stickery that any amunal who passes nearby is likely to become distremely entangled.

Chubbified: Chubby (although Mooses now consider it more politically correct to use the phrase "differently weighted.")

Deceptions (see Extra Sensory Deceptions)

Demember: remember (over and over again, from now on!)

Distremely: extremely

Drowndify: to drown

Dwarfy: of, about, concerning, referencing, referring or pertaining to, dwarfs.

Extra Sensory Deceptions: Special, sneaky, magical, telepathical and thoroughly reprehensible witchly powers.

Filthified: repulsively and disgustingly unclean

Glop (see Wudgies of Glop)

Incarceration: incarnation. Mooses believe that after they die, they can move their moosely souls into other amunal bodies. They call this re-incarceration. If they are very good, they can eventually give up being re-incarcerated, and get to be Everywhere at Once.

Never Afterwords: A standard ending for Moose Tales. It means that the story is over, and there are no more words to say about that!

Snaggled: intricately and thoroughly entangled

Unconshable: unconscious

Wudgies of Glop: Wudgies are little ugly gnarley blobs. Glop is any mysterious, disgusting, foul-smelling sticky stuff. Wudgies of glop are things you do not want to look at, let alone have in your hair! Yug!

Far away in the Northern Piney Woods there lives a storyteller named Maynard Moose. Every full moon in the forest, the animals come from near and far to hear him tell the old Mother Moose Tales, handed down so long ago. Young and old, big and small, fur and feather, the woodland creatures gather round and settle down on moss and branch and log to listen …

Did you ever hear a story that would go on and on,
and when you would get to the end you would
scratch your hairs and ask yourself, "Gee, what was
that all about?" And no matter how much you would
ask yourself, you still would not know? Well, here is a
story just like that! It is called Rapunzel and the
Seven Dwarfs.

Once upon a time, a long, long time ago ...

… there was a girl named Punzel
with long, long goldie hair.

Her hair was so long that it drag out from behind of her along the ground. It get dragged through mud puddles, and kids run over it on their bicycles, and it become distremely" filthified"—all full of sticks and twigs and little nastified wudgies of glop".

This was driving Punzel bananas! So one day, she decide to go to the witch's place to see if there was some kind of magic spell or gel that could keep her hairs clean.

The witch tried everything.

She tried spells

and she tried gels

and even a beehive hairdo.

But nothing worked, so instead she locked Punzel away in a tall, tall tower to keep her hairs from dragging on the ground.

Every day the witch would come to the bottom of the tower, and she would say:

"Punzel, Punzel, goldie fair,
Punzel, Punzel, let down the hair!"

And Punzel would let down her hair, and the witch would climb up and give her something to eat.

Well, one day, there come along a handsome prince, riding on a snow-white moose—a noble beast! And the prince peek out from behind a tree, and he see how the witch call up to Punzel and how she climb up the hairs and then back down again. So when the witch go away, the prince decide he is going to try the same thing.

The handsome prince, he tiptoe to the bottom of the tower, and he say it real quiet, 'cause he don't want the witch to hear him and turn him into a toad or something:

"Punzel, Punzel, goldie fair,
Punzel, punzel, let down the hair!"

But he don't say the words loud enough for Punzel to hear him real good. Her think him say: "Let down a pear." So she fling a big juicy pear out the window. SPLOT!

It hit the prince right on the shoe! He get out his little monogrammed princely hankie, and he wipe off the shoe, and then he try again:

"Punzel, Punzel, goldie fair,
Punzel, Punzel, let down the hair!"

But this time, Punzel sneeze just when he say "hair." And she think he say, "Let down your chair!" So she fling a big heavy chair out the window.

The chair hit the prince on the head, and he was knocked unconshable*! All of his previous incarcerations* fly by his eyeballs. When he wake up again, he try one more time:

"Punzel, Punzel, goldie fair,
Punzel, Punzel, let down the hair!"

This time Punzel hear him real good. Her let the hair all the way down, and the handsome prince start to climb up. But the prince, he was a little bit chubbified❝. The prince, he weigh five hundred and twelve pounds! The handsome prince was so heavy, when he start to climb up the hairs, he flip Punzel right out of the window! Her go sailing through the air and land in the duck pond. SPLASH!

Well, about that time, the seven dwarfs come by, on their way home from digging gold in the mountain. There was Clumsy, Snoozy, Cheerful, Fearful, Hyper, Hungry, Grizelda, Ambidextrous, and sometimes Bewildered..... *There were eight or nine seven dwarfs.*

So the eight or nine seven dwarfs see Punzel in the duck pond, and they do not want her to drowndify❞ herself—no! So they haul her out of the duck pond, and when Punzel tell them about how she has been locked up in the tower, the dwarfies decide to hide her away so the witch can't find her. 'Cause they are very worried the witch will become distremely angrified❞ when she find out that Punzel has runned away.

So through the forest they go, they go! Through the forest they go! Until Punzel's long, long goldie hair get all snaggled❝ up in a branglebush❝, and she is stuck fast and cannot move. Well, the only way to set her free is to cut her hairs off, so they shave Punzel bald as a bowling ball!

Well, just then the full moon start to rise. And the full moon, shining on the top of Punzel's head, make a little magic mirror there, like a shiny crystal ball. The dwarfies all gather round in a circle, and they say:

"Mirror, mirror on Punzel's head,
Is the witch alive or dead?"

And a picture of the witch float into view. She is distremely angrified, hopping up and down, smashing teacups and crockeries and kicking the cat. "Run away from me, will you, Punzel?" she yell. "Well, I'll fix you!"

"Quick! Quick!" say the dwarfies, and they lead Punzel away through the forest until they get to their little dwarfy" hovel, and there they lock the door.

Next morning, bright and early, off again go Clumsy, Snoozy, Cheerful, Fearful, Hyper, Hungry, Grizelda, Ambidextrous, and sometimes Bewildered, to dig gold in the mountain. "Now you be careful, Punzel," they say. "You stay inside and don't open the door!"

But meanwhile, the witch disguise herself as an old rhinocerous and come through the forest with a wheelbarrow full of poisoned watermelons. And every time she lose the way, she use her magical extra sensory deceptions❝:

"Mirror, mirror, on a stick—
Show me the dwarfies' house real quick!"

And off on a new path she would go.

Finally she get to the dwarfy hovel and knock on the door with the fake rhino horn—Bonk! Bonk! Punzel peek out the window. "Hello?"
"Hello," say the witch. "It's me, the friendly forest rhinocerous. Would you like a bite of one of my poisoned—oops!—I mean, tasty watermelons?"

"Oh boy! Oh boy!" say Punzel. "Watermelons is my favorite fruits! Yum!"
And her take a big bite of watermelon and fall down dead!

But don't worry—she was not really dead. She take such a big bite of
watermelon that it stick in her throat and she do not swallow it all the
way. So instead of being dead she just fell into an endless poison-
watermelon sleep.

Well, when the dwarfies come back from digging gold in the mountain and find Punzel unconshable in an endless sleep, they do not know what to do ... Everybody is sad, even Cheerful.

But pretty soon the dwarfies get an idea. They put her in a big glass box and charge all the amunals" twenty-five cents to come and see her.

All the forest amunals line up to have a look.

Well, the Sleeping Punzel Museum is a big success! Dwarfies don't have to dig for gold no more. Clumsy, Snoozy, Cheerful, Fearful, Hyper, Hungry, Grizelda, Ambidextrous, and sometimes Bewildered live on Easy Street!

But one day who should come along once more but the handsome prince, riding on the snow-white moose. And the moose did not look where it was going and trip over the glass case and smash it to smithereens!

Punzel wake up. She cough out the piece of watermelon! And when she see the noble, kindly, handsome moose leaning over her, she give him big kiss on the nose. "My hero!" say Punzel. And Punzel and the moose ride off into the sunrise. And they lived happily for never afterwords".

And as for the handsome prince, he go marry the witch and they live in the tall, tall tower happily for never afterwords. And as for the dwarfies, they go back to digging gold in the mountain: Clumsy, Snoozy, Cheerful, Fearful, Hyper, Hungry, Grizelda, Ambidextrous, and sometimes Bewildered for never afterwords.

And the moral of that story is, if you have long, long goldie hairs that drag out from behind of you along the ground, then you should always … um … The moral of that story is, if you get flipped out a window and land in the duck pond, you should always demember" that … um … you should demember … um Let's see … The moral of that story is … there ain't no moral to some stories at all!